The Attic Mice

THE
ATTIC MICE

Ethel Pochocki

Pictures by
DAVID CATROW

Henry Holt and Company ◆ *New York*

Published by Henry Holt and Company, Inc.,
115 West 18th Street, New York, New York 10011.
Published in Canada by Fitzhenry & Whiteside Limited,
195 Allstate Parkway, Markham, Ontario L3R 4T8.

Library of Congress Cataloging-in-Publication Data
Pochocki, Ethel.
The attic mice / Ethel Pochocki ; illustrated by David Catrow.
Summary: Recounts the adventures of a family of mice as they go
shopping in the humans' kitchen, discover useful items in the attic,
and celebrate Christmas.
ISBN 0-8050-1298-2
[1. Mice—Fiction.] I. Catrow, David, ill. II. Title.
PZ7.P7495At 1990
[Fic]—dc20 90-32064

Henry Holt books are available at special discounts
for bulk purchases for sales promotions, premiums,
fund-raising, or educational use. Special editions
or book excerpts can also be created to specification.

First Edition

Printed in the United States of America
on acid-free paper. ∞

1 3 5 7 9 10 8 6 4 2

To Arnold and Gertrude with love
                            —*E.P.*

To Deborah, for all your
love and support
                    —*D.C.*